O'BRIEN flyers

Can YOU spot the aeroplane hidden in the story?

For Noreen and Keith

WES MAGEE: A full-time author since 1989, Wes is a former primary school teacher and head teacher at large schools in England. He has published eighty books for young readers – poetry, fiction, play scripts, and picture books, as well as four collections of poetry for adults. His work has been featured on TV and radio. He lives in a village on the North Yorkshire Moors.

MARGARET SUGGS: Originally from Atlanta, Georgia, Margaret now lives in Ireland and teaches illustration, graphic design and history of art in Ballyfermot College. Her illustrations have appeared in books in Ireland, France and the US.

BLUE, WHERE ARE YOU?

Wes Magee

Illustrated by Margaret Suggs

THE O'BRIEN PRESS
DUBLIN

First published 2007 by The O'Brien Press Ltd,
12 Terenure Road East, Rathgar, Dublin 6, Ireland.
Tel: +353 1 4923333; Fax: +353 1 4922777
E-mail: books@obrien.ie
Website: www.obrien.ie

ISBN: 978-1-84717-009-5

British Library Cataloguing-in-Publication Data
Magee, Wes, 1939-
Blue, where are you? - (Flyers series)
1. Pets - Juvenile fiction 2. Moving, Household - Juvenile
fiction 3. Children's stories
I. Title
823.9'14[J]

1 2 3 4 5 6 7 8 9 10
07 08 09 10 11 12

The O'Brien Press receives
assistance from

arts
council
schomhairle
ealaíon

Typesetting, editing, layout, design: The O'Brien Press Ltd
Illustrations: Margaret Suggs
Printing: Cox & Wyman Ltd

11 NOV 2007

CHAPTER 1

The Old Farm House

In the middle of winter
the Watkins family moved into
the The Old Farm House high on
the moors.

The Old Farmhouse

Dad carried in Blue, the family cat. He put the cat basket down on the flagstone floor of the kitchen.

'Brrr! It's so cold in here,' said Mum. She gave a **shiver**. 'The first thing we have to do is to light the boiler and get some heat into the house.'

Dad opened the cat basket.
Blue **sniffed** for a moment and
then jumped out.

'This is your new home,' said
Jo, stroking Blue's silky coat.

Blue was a grey-blue colour. Her paws were white and so was the tip of her tail. She had long whiskers.

Jo and her young brother, Josh, watched as Blue sniffed her way around the kitchen.

'She knows it's not home,' Josh said.

Blue padded slowly and softly from room to room.

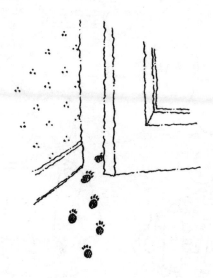

She **explored** The Old Farm House while Jo, Josh, Mum and Dad carried in toys, tables, TVs and towels from the van.

Later that afternoon, as light was fading, the family sat down to their meal in the kitchen of The Old Farm House.

'Blue!' called Jo. 'It's dinner time!'

But Blue didn't appear.

'Blue,' shouted Josh. 'Blue, where are you?'

No Blue.

'She'll be exploring,' said Mum. 'Don't worry, she'll turn up in her own good time. She'll come for her dinner. Cats **always** do.'

But Blue didn't turn up. Her dinner lay **untouched** in her special bowl on the kitchen's flagstone floor.

CHAPTER TWO

Blue, Where Are You?

While Mum and Dad unpacked,
Jo and Josh searched for Blue.

In the hall
they peeped
behind an old
hatstand.
Something
squeaked, and
then **scuttled**
away.

'What was
that?'
whispered
Josh.

'A **mouse**,' said Jo. 'And it had a really long tail!'

The children stood in the cold hall.

'Blue,' called Jo. 'Where are you?'

... Blue ... Blue ... Blue ... her voice echoed.

But Blue didn't appear.

Jo and Josh **clomped** up the
bare wooden stairs.

On the landing, a clock struck
five.

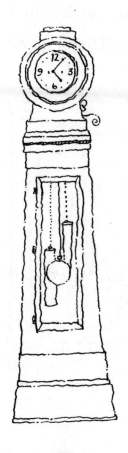

Outside, it was already dark.
An icy wind **whistled** around The Old
Farm House.

'Let's look in here,' said Jo, and she
pushed open a bedroom door. The
door creaked. They looked inside.

'Blue!' called the girl.

The children saw bed ends, mattresses and piles of pillows. A bare bulb was hanging from the ceiling.

'It's not like home, is it?' said Josh, quietly.

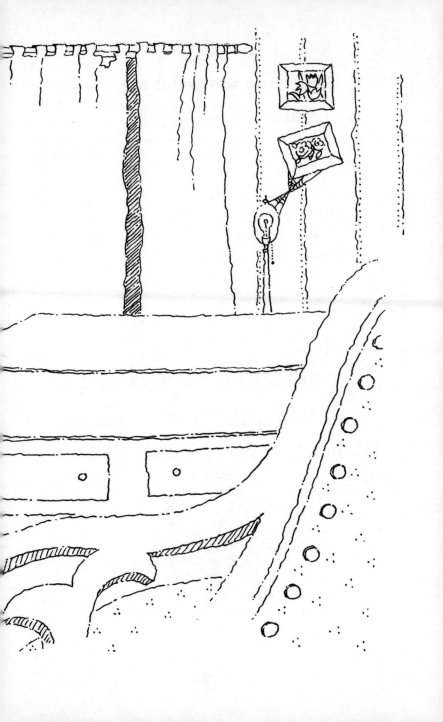

Something **ran** across the floorboards.

'What was *that*?' whispered Josh.

'A **wolf spider**,' said Jo. 'And just about the biggest I've ever seen!'

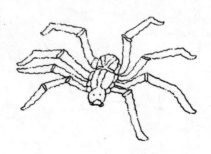

The children searched and searched for their missing pet.

'Blue!' called Jo. 'Where are you?'

No Blue.

In the next room they found Mum and Dad making up beds.

'Have you seen Blue?' asked Jo.

'No,' said Mum. 'She's not in here.'

Jo and Josh searched another bedroom, then the box room, and then the bathroom. There was **no sign** of their cat.

No Blue.

CHAPTER THREE

In the Attic

'Let's look in the attic,' said Jo.
'Perhaps Blue will be there.'

She pointed up a narrow
staircase.

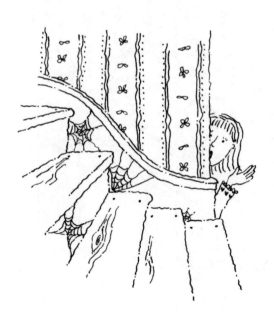

'It's dark up there,' said Josh uncertainly. 'It looks a bit **scary**.'

Jo started up the staircase. Josh followed his sister. The old stairs creaked.

'Blue!' called Jo, as she stepped into the attic.

Thin beams of moonlight shone through a cobwebby skylight. They cast **spooky shadows** on the wooden beams.

'Blue, where are you?' called Jo.

Something fluttered in the dusty gloom.

'What was *that*?' whispered Josh.

'It could have been a bird,' said Jo. 'Or a **bat**!'

Josh shivered.

'It's not like home, is it?' he said.

'Blue! Blue!' called Jo. 'Blue, where are you?'

But Blue didn't appear.

Blue wasn't in the attic.

CHAPTER FOUR

The Barn

Downstairs, the children found
Mum and Dad unrolling a carpet
in the hall.

'Have you found her?' asked Mum.

'No,' said Jo and Josh.

'I hope she's not **run away**,' said Mum.

She stopped working and looked at Jo and Josh.

'You know, sometimes a cat will try to find its way back to its old home,' Mum told them.

'Don't worry, she'll turn up,'
said Dad, and he gave a laugh.

But Jo and Josh didn't laugh.

They looked sad.

'Perhaps Blue went out
through the cat flap,' said Mum.

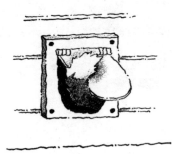

'Take the torch and look
outside. But put on your coats
first, it's **really cold** out there!'

Jo found the torch and opened the back door. Outside, the winter wind was **wild**. It whistled in the treetops. Clouds scudded across the moon.

'Here we go,' said Jo, and the beam from the torch cut through the darkness.

The children hurried across the cobblestone yard.

'It's **freezing** cold,' said Jo. 'I hope Blue has found shelter somewhere.'

A shadow **crept** along the wall of an old stone barn.

'What was *that*?' whispered Josh.

'It could have been a **fox**,' said Jo. 'Or a **badger**!'

Josh shivered
and shivered.

'Let's look in
the barn,' said Jo.

The beam
from the torch flashed around the
old barn.

The children saw bales of hay,
a broken ladder, piles of plastic sacks,
and farm tools.

'Blue!' called Jo. 'Blue!'

'Blue, where are you?' called Josh.

But Blue didn't appear.

Blue wasn't in the barn.

CHAPTER FIVE

Sleep Tight

That evening the children got
ready for bed. There was still no
sign of Blue.

'Your first night in The Old
Farm House,' said Mum. 'Isn't it
exciting?'

'No,' said Jo. 'There's no Blue.'

Josh felt **sad**. Sad and cold. He
pulled the duvet up under his chin.

'It's not like home, Mum,' he said quietly.

'It will be,' said Mum. 'It will be. It **always** feels strange in a new place.'

'Tomorrow will be better,' said Dad. 'Just you wait and see!' And he winked at Josh.

'Goodnight,' said Mum, 'sleep tight.' She switched off the light.

All night an icy wind whistled across the moors. Tree branches **tapped** and **scratched** at the bedroom windows.

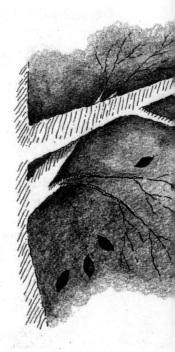

In the morning Jo woke up and saw a strange **glow** on the bedroom ceiling. She jumped out of bed and ran to the window.

'Josh!' she shouted. 'Look!'

'What is it?' mumbled Josh.

'Snow!' shouted Jo. 'Snow! It's
a **white world**!'

Jo and Josh gazed from the
bedroom window.

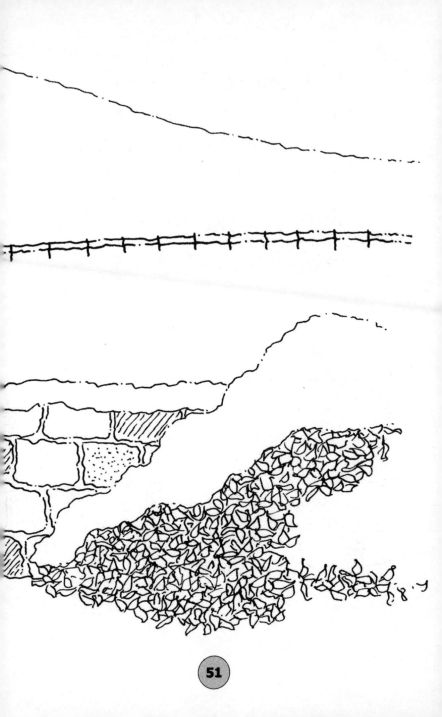

The icy wind had died away, and deep snow lay across the moors. Everything was silent and still. A pale sun shone faintly in the ice-blue sky.

'**Snow**!' said Jo, excitedly.

'Snow!' whispered Josh.

CHAPTER SIX

A Big Surprise

'Jo! Josh!' called Mum from downstairs. 'Come and see what's here!'

The children **clattered** down the bare stairs and ran along the hall.

In the kitchen it felt warm. Dad
was feeding coal into the old boiler. It
popped and **pinged** and **sizzled**
with heat.

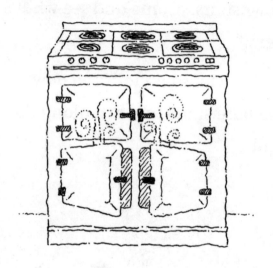

'Surprise!' said Mum, with a big
smile.

'What is it?' asked Jo.

'There,' said Mum, pointing.
'Look!'

Lying in a box on a pile of
Dad's old sweatshirts was …
a kitten. A tiny kitten with its eyes
closed.

'It's … it's … ' began Josh.

'I know,' said Mum, and gave him a hug.

Then, who came pushing her way through the cat flap?

Blue!

And in her mouth she carried a **second** kitten.

Jo, Josh, Mum and Dad
watched as Blue lay down beside
her two kittens and **licked** them
again and again.

And did she purr?

She certainly did.

She purred and purred and purred.

'Blue!' cried Jo, kneeling beside the cat.

'Blue, you've come back!' cried Josh, kneeling beside his sister.

'What a **wonderful** house-warming present,' said Mum with a wide smile. 'Two new kittens.'

'See,' said Dad with a laugh, 'I **told** you tomorrow would be better. And it is!'

It wasn't long before the radiators in The Old Farm House were **ticking** as heat spread to every room. Outside there was cold snow, but inside it was

warm. *And* there were two new kittens!

'Well, Jo,' said Mum. 'What do you think of The Old Farm House now?'

'It's **great**,' said Jo. 'It's just great.'

'And what about you, Josh?' asked Mum. 'What do *you* think?'

Josh thought for a moment.

Then he said, 'It feels ... it feels just like home, Mum. And best of all, Blue's **come back**!'